THE NOT SO SILLY BUTTERFLY

By Barbara Hollander with Joshua Hollander
Illustrated by Jody Rosen

Xlibris Publishing

To order additional copies of this book, contact:
Xlibris
844-714-8691
www.Xlibris.com
Orders@Xlibris.com

ISBN: 978-1-4363-4708-2 (sc)
ISBN: 978-1-6698-0875-6 (e)

Print information available on the last page

Rev. date: 01/25/2022

To Ruthie, with much love, hugs & kisses

To Jim & Justin, for your support & encouragement

Monica the Monarch Butterfly lived on the beautiful island of St. Martin. Her black and orange wings glistened in the bright Caribbean sun. She had a heart-shaped face, a warm smile and sparkling brown eyes. Monica was brave and curious. But most of all, Monica was a dreamer who longed to see the world beyond the Butterfly Farm.

The Butterfly Farm was near the colorful homes of Orient Bay. It had delicious milkweeds, smooth leaves and red flowers. The Farm also had a pond with golden fish that swam calmly in the cool, running water. Monica had loved the Farm ever since she wiggled out of her cocoon. But each day, Monica grew more curious about the rest of the Island.

Throughout the day, visitors came from all over the world to visit the butterflies. Big buses brought women with yellow straw hats, men in blue caps and children wearing bathing suits and smiles.

"Why do so many people come to St. Martin?" asked Monica.

"They come to see the Island," answered her mother.

"I want to see the Island," responded Monica.

"Silly Monica," said her mother. "Butterflies don't see islands. Butterflies stay on the Farm."

In the morning, Monica flew to a wooden table full of overripe oranges, watermelons and bananas. The oranges were her favorite breakfast treat. She would sit and lick their sweet, tangy juice.

"I want to see a person drinking orange juice," said Monica to her sister.

"Silly Monica," said her sister. "Butterflies don't watch people drink juice. Butterflies stay on the Farm."

At noon, the sun shone directly overhead. It was the hottest time of the day. Monica liked to hide in the cool shade of the dark green leaves. Sometimes, Monica would look at the warm, yellow circle in the sky.

"I want to fly as high as the sun," said Monica to her brother.

"Silly Monica," said her brother. "Butterflies don't fly to the sun. Butterflies stay on the Farm."

At night, Monica liked to fall asleep to the soothing sound of the Ocean.

"What song is the water playing tonight?" Monica asked her father.

"It is the dance of the waves tickling the beach," answered her father, as he reached out and began tickling his daughter.

"I want to see the beach dance," laughed Monica.

"Silly Monica," said her father. "Butterflies don't see beaches. Butterflies stay on the Farm."

One day, a little girl with strawberry blond hair came to the Butterfly Farm. The girl's backpack was covered with orange and black butterflies. Monica flew towards them, eager to make new friends. But as Monica landed on the backpack, she realized that the butterflies were only painted pictures.

Monica sat on the backpack, as the little girl winded around the dirt path. She sat on the backpack, as the little girl crossed over a wooden bridge. Monica even sat on the backpack, as the girl left the Farm through a creaking door. For the first time, Monica was outside the Farm.

At first, Monica was scared because she had never been outside the Farm. Then, Monica remembered her dream of flying to the sun.   She soared higher and faster than ever before and landed on a bush at Paradise Peak. Monica looked at the tree-covered mountains that led to a sparkling sea.

"It's a beautiful view," said a scratchy voice behind her.

Monica jumped. She turned around, but no one was there.

"Who said that?" whispered Monica.

"I did," said the brown, scaly lizard below her.

Monica eyed the lizard ready to pounce and flew away just in time.

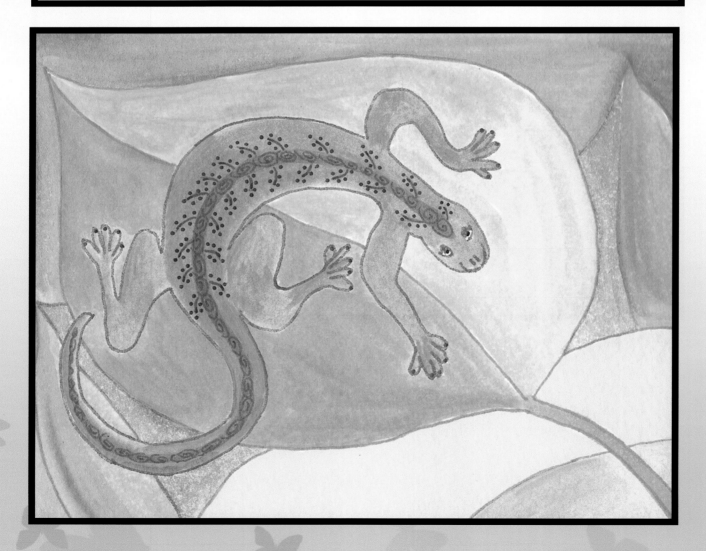

Soon, Monica arrived at one of St. Martin's salt ponds. She landed on a small patch of flowers that overlooked the pond.

"Who are you?" she asked the bird in the water.

"I am a Great Blue Heron," answered the bird. "And I am also the Keeper of the Pond."

"What does the Keeper do?" asked Monica.

"I guard the salt," explained the Heron. "Long ago, people came to this Island and took salt out of the ponds. Now, it is my job to keep the salt in the water."

Monica smiled. "Thank you," she said, "for telling me why many people came to this Island."

Monica left and flew towards the Sea. She passed green mountains, yellow fields, and breezy, blue waters until she came to the city of Marigot. A narrow, winding road with a single row of cars sat next to the city's marketplace. Monica flew by shiny silver bracelets, dolls in colorful dresses and hand drawn paintings.

As Monica neared the last booth, the smell of fresh fruit filled the air. She flew to a stand with rainbow colored jars. Monica watched a boy named Raffi sip his orange juice. Raffi saw the beautiful Monarch Butterfly staring at his glass. He pushed the juice in Monica's direction, and she began to drink.

"Thank you," she whispered, as she flew far away from the city.

The sun was setting and evening was coming. As she looked for a place to sleep, Monica thought of her father and his beach songs. Then, Monica heard a song of her own. It was the sound of the Sea mixed with the beat of drums. She flew towards the music and found the Belair Beach Hotel near Little Bay.

Monica rested on a bush with dark red flowers. She gently fell asleep, lulled by the sounds of the waves gently hugging the shore and the songs from the nearby Gingerbread Café. When Monica awoke the next day, she heard a different sound. It was the barking of a dog named China Rose. The dog was standing near a palm tree that pointed to the open glimmering Sea.

Monica watched the waves wash over the sand and felt the sun's heat warm her wings. It was a beautiful morning, and yet sadness filled her heart. Monica missed her family, and she missed the Butterfly Farm. After breakfast, Monica knew that she would fly home. She had flown to St. Martin's highest point, learned why people came so long ago, watched a boy drink his orange juice and visited the beaches. Monica had seen the Island. She was not a silly butterfly, after all.

DID YOU KNOW?

Butterflies are insects with six jointed legs and four wings.

Butterflies develop in four stages:

1) **EGG:** A female Monarch Butterfly can lay between 300 and 400 eggs. Each egg is laid on a single milkweed leaf and takes between 3 and 12 days to hatch. Warm weather makes the eggs hatch faster!

2) **LARVA:** This is the caterpillar stage. The caterpillar's job is to eat lots of leaves. It only takes 3 days for a caterpillar to double its size.

3) **CHRYSALIS:** The caterpillar forms a chrysalis, or pupa. It stays in this pouch for 12 to 15 days.

4) **BUTTERFLY:** The Butterfly comes out of the chrysalis and can eventually soar into the sky.

The whole cycle from egg to butterfly takes about 4 weeks.

Monarch Butterflies are amazing fliers. They travel, or migrate, great distances of up to 3,000 miles. Monarch Butterflies migrate to avoid cold weather and to find food, such as milkweed leaves.

Monarch Butterflies can be found in many places, including the United States, Southern Canada, Australia, Asia...and of course, St. Martin.

The Butterfly Farm in St. Martin opened for visitors in 1994. It is one of the many butterfly farms and gardens found throughout the world. Visit a nearby butterfly farm and wear bright colors to make the butterflies land on you!

About the Authors

Barbara Hollander graduated with a B.A. in Economics from the University of Michigan and Summa Cum Laude from New York University's Graduate Economics Program. She is the author of *Managing Money* and *Raising Money*, part of the Heinemann Library Life Skill Set Series and the children's book *Henry the Great's First Adventure.* Barbara is a consultant with the Educational Testing Service, a course writer and online content developer with Knowledge Learning Corporation and a regular contributor for newspapers and magazines including *NJJN* and *Kid Zone.* She is also a board member of the Literacy Connections Committee that promotes literacy in the special needs school, P.G. Chambers. Barbara lives in New Jersey with her husband and their three children.

Barbara is honored to write her first picture book with her eleven-year-old son, Joshua. **Joshua Hollander** is a gifted writer, often called "The Master of Description." He is both a Dan Gutman Essay Contest Winner and a Youth Author Second Place Winner in *Stories for Children Magazine.* Joshua was also chosen to participate in Thomas Edison's Wendy Maas Writing Workshop.

About the Illustrator

Jody Sweet Rosen was born outside of San Francisco, and has lived in Carmel & the Big Sur Mountains. In 1985, Jody moved to the Caribbean Island of St. Maarten with her husband, Jim, and son, Justin. She built a small Café and successfully ran it for six years. In 1991, Jody began painting, inspired by the turquoise waters and vegetation of the Island. Her work is on display at the Gingerbread Café at the Belair Beach Hotel. Jody also features her artwork on small canvases for tote bags and does larger pieces on stretched canvas. Currently, Jody owns a small convenience store and sells timeshares at the Belair Beach Hotel. She enjoys painting, glazing ceramics, swimming,running and dance.

Printed in the United States
by Baker & Taylor Publisher Services